The Seven Magic Marbles

Ranald Macdonald

Illustrated by

William Simpson

Beamore Books

For Teresa

First published 1999 by Beamore Books
11 Chippendale Glen,
Bangor,
Co Down,
N Ireland,
BT20 4NU

Reprinted 2001

Text copyright 1999 Ranald Macdonald
Illustrations copyright 1999 William Simpson

The rights of Ranald Macdonald and William Simpson to be identified as the author and illustrator of this work have been asserted by them in accordance with the Copyright, Designs and Patents Act 1988

ISBN 0 9535589 3 2

Designed by Ken Simpson
Printed in Ireland by
Colourbooks

The Seven Magic Marbles

Contents

1. The Princess....................................1

2. The Feathers..................................18

3. The Two Crabs...............................25

4. The Ferryman...............................31

5. The Forgotten Forest.................41

6. The Dwarf King..........................52

7. The Seven Magic Marbles..........73

1 The Princess

Grandpa opened his hand. There, in the palm, lay seven marbles, glowing softly in the lamp-light.

"Oh, yes," he said quietly, "there is a story to these. Indeed there is. Come closer and I'll tell you."

I moved up to his side and gazed at the marbles. They seemed like worlds, each one with its oceans and continents. Grandpa stared at them, the way a fortune-teller might peer into a crystal ball.

"They hardly shine at all any more," he went on.

"What do you mean?" I asked.

"They used to have a light all of their own," he said, in a faraway voice. "That was the point!"

"Do you mean – they could light up a room?"

"Oh, more than that." He raised his eyes and looked into the distance. "A castle," he said, and nodded. "Yes, a castle. But that's not the most important thing."

"What is then?"

His eyes grew moist. He seemed to be remembering something.

"When the first rays of the morning sun

touched the seven magic marbles any sick person who saw it could be healed!"

I glanced at the marbles. I hoped to see signs of their magic.

"How do you know, Grandpa?" I asked. "Have you ever seen it happen?"

"It's so long ago," he answered. "I can hardly remember it all. You might not believe it anyway."

"Go on, tell me!" I pleaded.

"Well, it's difficult to explain. It happened in the days before there were towns and houses like ours, with everything that we know in them. In those days forests were dark and unknown. People understood that magic existed and were not disbelievers the way they are now. I myself knew magic kingdoms and saw what happened there."

"What did happen there, Grandpa? And what were the magic marbles for?"

"I will tell you. But you must be patient because the story starts a long time ago and is hard to remember –

I was young like the morning in those days, and daring. One day I went further into the forest than I was used to, and came to a cave I did not know.

I went in and saw a magical sight. The cave was flickering and flashing with the light of thousands of crystals, which must have been there since the beginning of time. The further I went into the cave, the more dazzling they became, until I felt my head grow dizzy and I fell down in a faint. There must have been a very strange magic working because when I woke up I was no longer the boy I had been when I had entered the cave. The magic in the cave had taken me into another time, and made me another person.

I knew who I was, nonetheless. I was a boy
called Berry, who lived with his mother in a poor
village. I was named after the fruits of the forest
because I was good at collecting them when
there was nothing else to eat. I knew, also, that

I made a living for my mother and myself by drawing water from the woodland springs and selling it in the parched streets below the castle.

It did not seem strange to me that I was another person, in another time. I felt as if Berry had always been my name.

But as I looked around me I was surprised to see the crystals in the cave had been crudely hacked away and their light was dimmed. Who had done this? I rushed out and saw two things. One was a lion, being led away in a cage on the back of a cart. It was a magnificent beast, with a thick, bushy mane and fiery eyes. The other was a beggar, running, in a limping kind of way, towards the town.

"What's going on?" I cried. "Where is that lion being taken, and what happened to the crystals in this cave?"

"The crystals?" repeated the man. "Oh, the Dwarf King's taken them to make his magic ornaments. And the lion is for him too. He will make a tame pet out of it. But strong enough to kill his enemies."

"That is a pity," I thought.

But the man went on excitedly, "Are you not

going up to the town? There is a great proclamation being read – a chance for any poor beggar to become a king!"

I followed him to the town and came to the
market square. The mighty castle loomed over
us. We were a great crowd that day. I was in

time to hear the proclamation, for the messenger came out shortly.

"You all know already," began the messenger, "that the king's daughter is sick, almost to the point of death."

"A shame," said the woman next to me. "And they wanted so much to have a child!"

I knew myself the story of the king and the queen and how they had longed to have a baby daughter to brighten their days. And when at last she had come, she had been more beautiful than the morning sun.

"For years now," went on the herald, " no one has been able to help her. The best doctors have been called. They have been promised great rewards. But it has been no use. Not one of them has ever seen such an illness before."

It was well known to everyone there: the little princess slept all the time and never heard the birds singing in the morning or saw the golden rays of the sun dancing around her bed.

"And yet," said the messenger, "there is one old man who has arrived at the castle, and he knows the answer!"

A gasp went up from the crowd.

"Will she be healed?" cried someone.

The messenger looked serious.

"There is a cure, the old man has told us. It is this: only when the dancing rays of the morning sun have touched the Seven Magic Marbles, only then shall the little princess be healed!"

"The Seven Magic Marbles!" exclaimed another man. "Where can they be found?"

"That is the problem," continued the messenger. "The Seven Magic Marbles are the property of the Dwarf King, and are to be found in his castle!"

"The Dwarf King!" cried several people at

once.

"Who in his right mind is going to get them there?!" said the woman next to me.

The messenger went on, "The old man has said that the Dwarf King keeps them as his dearest treasure. Now the king has sent his messengers into every part of the land to find the Castle of the Dwarf King. But they cannot find it. The Castle is hidden in the Forgotten Forest. And no one remembers where that is."

The crowd fell silent, pondering over this news.

"Here is the proclamation," spoke the messenger. "Whoever can find the Castle of the Dwarf King and bring back the Seven Magic Marbles, will have the hand of the princess in marriage and half the kingdom for his own!"

The crowd gasped again in excitement.

"I could try!" shouted one toothless old man.

"And me!" called another, only slightly younger.

The man I had met in the forest was standing behind me. "You see?" he said. "A beggar could become a king."

"Let it be known," went on the messenger, "the best minds in the land have already tried. But not one can remember the place of the Forgotten Forest. Though they have spent all their money on maps and magic tricks, no one has come close. Yet it is possible that someone might still succeed. If that one is here, let him show himself to the king!"

The crowd dispersed after that. I think they all knew the task was too much for them.

I don't know why I thought myself different. I just could not help thinking of the poor princess, lying there in her bed, unable to open her eyes. I had this overwhelming feeling in me that I could do it! I had no right to think it, but I did.

It was two days before I summoned up the

courage to go into the castle. I took my water bottles with me, as if for an excuse.

It was the first time I have ever stood before a king. He smiled at me, indulgently, as if he thought it was funny that a boy like me should come before him. So I offered him some water, and said it came from the purest spring in the forest, which it did.

"It is very good," he said, and looked at me thoughtfully. "If you can bring water like this, then perhaps you can do more."

"Oh, please, Your Majesty, let me try!" I cried.

"You know something about healing, then?" he replied.

"Your Majesty, I only know this – whenever I have looked into the face of my mother when she has been sick in bed, I have known straightaway where to find the herb in the forest that could make her well again."

"I see. This is not a question of herbs, of course."

"No, sire, but I feel sure that if I could look into the face of your daughter, I would then know where to search for the Magic Marbles!"

"Not many people are allowed to see her," answered the king. "But I think, in your case, I will let you do as you ask."

My heart positively jumped and the king led me up the winding stairway to his daughter's chamber. I looked into her face, and oh! so pitiful it was, still and unmoving, but beautiful nonetheless. But unfortunately I did not know straightaway where to search for the Magic Marbles. Yet I did not lose heart.

I whispered in her ear, "Oh, princess, even if it costs me my life I will find them for you!" And as I said it I could swear that for a moment her eyelids flickered.

I went back to the woods and thought very hard about the promise I had made. Then, as I knelt before the spring to draw some water, I saw the reflection of the princess herself, but not as she was now. I saw her, as she had been before the illness, a young girl, radiant as the morning sun. She spoke to me, saying, "Berry, fetch me the little orange flower of the wood-herb to put by my pillow while you are away." Then the water shook and her reflection vanished.

I knew exactly what flower she meant and it did not take me long to find it. Once I held it safely in my hands, I went back to the castle. The king, who was kind to me still, let me put the flower on the princess's pillow. As I did so, I saw her eyelids flicker again. But there was nothing I could do to wake her up.

2) The Feathers

Grandpa stopped.

"Wasn't it strange to be like someone else?" I asked.

"To be someone else," he corrected me. "No, I don't think so. I took it for granted somehow."

"Do you think you were dreaming?"

Grandpa thought for a minute.

"No, everything that happened was as real as this is now, with you and me sitting here. I was so involved in what I was doing I didn't even stop to think about it."

"It must have been magic though, Grandpa."

"Oh, that it was – that's for sure! But not just make-believe."

"Did you find the Seven Magic Marbles?"

"Slowly, now – there is a long way to go before I come to that part. Just wait and listen."

I settled in close beside Grandpa, and rested my head on his arm. He went on with his story–

Now when I came out of the palace – I was the boy Berry, remember – I saw an old woman sitting in the sun outside the kitchen door. She was plucking a hen. I looked closer and saw that it was a moorhen – a fine, plump bird.

Something made me ask her, "Grandma – are you very old?"

She cackled with laughter.

"Me? Old? My child, I'm as old as this castle, I do believe. I remember its last bricks being laid!"

"Then could you tell me where to find the Forgotten Forest?"

"The Forgotten Forest? The Forgotten Forest... Well, now, as a matter of fact – no. Oh, dear, so many things get forgotten about. Or lost. Then when you try to remember them, and at last you do, you wonder how you could ever have forgotten.

"Now where did I put that old brown sack?"

She looked around for the bag to put the feathers in. I could see it peeping out from under the pile of feathers, and I handed it to her.

"Now I remember what I wanted to say," she
went on. "This fat hen is for the king's table. If
you can fetch me the sweetest, freshest herbs of
the forest to stuff it with, then I might be able to
help you."

Well, that was my trade, of course, so I will-

ingly went to look for the herbs. For some reason I went back to the area around the crystal
cave. Everything was normally so full of life
there. But this time, the ground looked parched
and dry. The flowers were withered and the
herbs were drooping. I looked into the cave out
of curiosity but before I could go in I heard the
very distant roar of a lion.

"Have they still not got that lion to the Dwarf
King's Castle?" I thought. "I would like to rescue
him!"

Then I also thought, if the Dwarf King had
destroyed the crystals in the cave, he must have
withered all the herbs around it as well, and I
was not happy with that. I thought there was
nothing good about him at all.

"If I can," I promised myself, "I will come back
here with the Seven Magic Marbles and make
everything well again!"

I had to go further into the forest to find herbs good enough for the king's table.

When I had them I went back to the old woman. She was sweeping up outside the kitchen door. She had packed all the feathers into her brown bag.

She breathed in the scent of the herbs and shut her eyes to savour it.

"These will do. They will do very well!" she said.

"Will you help me then?" I asked.

"Oh, yes – that."

She stooped down and pulled out a handful of feathers from her bag.

"Do you see how soft they are? No ordinary feathers are as soft as that. I'm going to stuff my pillow with them. Then I will be able to dream again! The reason they are as soft as they are, is that the bird who owned them had flown over the Forgotten Forest. Look, I'll save three of them to fly on the wind. They'll fly like no others!"

The old woman cast the feathers into the air. Although it was a still day, they seemed to find an invisible breeze and floated up into the sky.

"You see? All you need to do is to follow them and they will lead you back to the Forgotten Forest. But be careful! The Dwarf King imprisons anyone who comes there in a pillar of stone!"

"Thank you, Grandma!" I cried, already following the drifting feathers away from the castle.

③ The Two Crabs

"Grandpa," I asked, "do you think the princess was really un- un-"

"Unconscious?"

"Yes. Or, was she awake a little bit?"

"As a matter of fact, I know – or someone told

me later – that when the moorhen was cooked in the herbs I had gathered, and the aroma came up to the princess's chamber, her eyelids flickered and she nearly came awake. But not quite."

"But you said you saw her in the stream. And that she spoke to you."

"Yes, that's right. It was the real princess I saw. Or rather her reflection. But I told you it was a kind of magic – it was all magic, everything that happened."

"Grandpa, do you think it was a fairy-tale world you were in?"

"Oh, yes. It was my home world. I mean Berry's. But it was a fairy-tale world too. And what happened next was definitely magic."

"Why? What was it?" I asked, excitedly.

"Well, I will tell you –

You see, I followed the feathers wherever they

drifted. It was lucky I had with me my own little pouch of bread and a small flask of water, because I actually went a long way. I did not know where I was any more. I think I must have come to many places that were forgotten – or nearly forgotten – but in each place I always met one last person who remembered it. So, you see, I didn't come to the Forgotten Forest.

And all the time, the feathers flew on ahead of me, like lucky charms floating on the wind. Sometimes they went swiftly, sometimes slowly.

At last I came as far as I could go. I was on the shore, with the green sea stretching out as far as I could see. And this was the difficult point – the feathers went on out across the water.

What was I going to do? Was I really meant to follow them? And how?

Now this is where the magic or enchantment came in, because a very strange thing hap-

pened. Two crabs came scurrying across the sand. They were as big as dinner plates, and pink, with tough shells. I should really say, they were as big as stepping-stones.

They were quite a comical pair, because each time one crab stood still, the other crab ran round it and waited at the front. They never seemed to end their game, or competition, or whatever it was. I had to laugh. But, to my surprise, I saw them go into the water and continue their strange manouevres there. This time they were swimming, one in front of the other, and so on. I could not help noticing they were going in the same direction as the feathers.

Now I did something I would never have dared to do in an ordinary sea, in an ordinary world. But I think I must have been somewhere near the Forgotten Forest because the water was different here. It was almost possible to stand on its surface. Perhaps my own heels were enchanted.

I got up onto the first crab's back, steadied myself, and stepped onto the second. They did not shake or bite or throw me off. I concentrated so hard, I lost sight of everything around me. The two crabs became my stepping-stones! One foot in front of the other, I walked across the sea!

I was so intent on keeping my balance I did not see anything except the three feathers dancing on, in the twilight air.

Then in the light of the twinkling stars my magical journey ended. We arrived at an island. I flopped down on the warm sand and fell asleep.

4 The Ferryman

When I woke up I was not quite sure if it was morning or afternoon. The sun seemed to be shining from all directions at once, as if it was in the middle of a thick, golden cloud. And the ground beneath my feet felt soft, a bit like some-

thing watery, or liquid. I could not see any forest,
but the feathers were still floating on the air.

"Welcome to the Island of Yesterday," said a
deep voice behind me. I whirled round. There

stood an old man with a long beard.

"Very few people come here," said the old man.

"Who are you, and why is it called the Island of Yesterday?" I asked.

"I am the Ferryman, and it is called Yesterday, because only when someone finds the Seven Magic Marbles and brings them back, will the island change its name. Then it will be called Tomorrow."

"Can you tell me how to find the Seven Magic Marbles?" I asked.

"I cannot tell that unless you climb into my boat and row for me."

"Row for you?"

"Oh, yes – to the land of the Forgotten Forest. You do want to go there, don't you?"

"I do! Of course I do! That's why I'm here!"

"Well, then," went on the old man, "I am the

Ferryman, but I am tired of rowing. If we go out a little way onto the water, with me rowing, will you take a turn?"

"Oh, yes!" I said eagerly.

The Ferryman led me round to the other side of the small island. We passed the two crabs as we went. They were still scurrying round each other. From this side of the island the sea looked dark and stormy. The Ferryman was unconcerned.

"Come along then," he said. "We have a long way to go."

Well, I climbed in and sat at the back of the boat. The Ferryman went forward, took up the oars, and rowed steadily. With every stroke we were taken further into the stormy seas. The clouds grew dark above us and the wind began to howl. Somehow, the little boat seemed to glide easily through the water.

Just when it looked at its roughest, and I could

see no land at all, the old man put down his oars and said, "Now it is your turn".

We changed places and I started to row. The boat began to rock and sway. The waves leapt higher than ever. I can tell you, I was scared! I tried to row as hard as I could, but we didn't seem to get anywhere. In fact, I felt sure we were going backwards.

At this stage, the boat was like a child's toy, being tossed up and down. Wind and waves pummeled us.

"How are we going to get there, with me row-ing?" I cried.

"Don't be scared," said the old man. "We will get there. I can assure you it's a pleasant rest for me not to have to row!"

"A pleasant rest!" I thought to myself. "He calls this a pleasant rest!" But I did not stop rowing.

At last, when I thought we'd been blown further backwards than we had gone forwards, I was ready to give up. But then the picture of the poor sick princess came into my mind, with the little orange flower resting on her pillow. And this thought gave' me new strength.

I rowed as hard as I could and began to think we were not going backwards so fast any more. To my amazement, the Ferryman said, "You may stop now. We are there."

"How can we be there?"

I shouted back. "We've been going backwards!"

"Look behind you," said the old man quietly.

I turned round and saw we'd reached a dark, grey shore. Looming over the shore, stretched an enormous forest.

"Let's go ashore now," said the Ferryman. "You did very well."

I stepped, thankfully, onto dry land. The first thing I saw when I looked down, were the three feathers, nestling between some twigs.

"The Forgotten Forest!" exclaimed the old man.

"Is the Dwarf King here?" I asked.

"He is, unless it's his time to go out into the world. But if you want to find him, you'll have to go through the Forest first. You'll have to be very careful there – it has giants in it. And not very nice ones."

"Giants? Do they really exist?"

"They do. Here. You're not at home any more, and things will seem very strange. You'll need help, of course, but there is no one who can help you when you get to the Dwarf King's Castle. The only thing you can do is look for the Moonstone. It will help you."

"The Moonstone?"

"Yes. You'll know it if you see it. Pick it up and keep it safe. It's the most important thing you could find. I won't tell you more. Good luck!"

And the old Ferryman rowed swiftly and silently back across the troubled waters.

5 The Forgotten Forest

"Grandpa," I asked, "did he really say giants?"

"Oh, yes."

"And did you believe him?"

"Well, by now I was ready to believe anything.
You see, I had journeyed further and further

away from home. Even for the boy Berry – and that was me of course – these things were strange. But this was a world of magic – totally and completely. I didn't disbelieve it. I was in it."

"Grandpa, I think the cave you went into was a story cave. Only when you went into it, you went into the story."

"Well, I hadn't thought of it that way. I still believe that whatever happened to me there really did happen. And I'll say why in a minute. But for now I think we have enough to deal with. The giants-"

"Oh, yes! Tell me about the giants!"

"All right. Just listen –

I had got to the Forgotten Forest. Well, it was very dark indeed. It had the look of a place that no one had ever visited. It was filled with a kind of soft moonlight that shone without there being any moon in the sky. I was not very surprised the place was forgotten.

But there were a few things I remembered. There were some berries I knew. They were like cousins of the ones I collected at home. I filled my pockets with two different kinds. I knew what they would do: one kind helped make you go to sleep. The other kept you awake when you wanted to go to sleep. The funny thing was that as soon as I had plucked the berries some new ones sprouted in their place. I had never seen anything grow so quickly.

When I looked at the ground beneath me, I discovered I could see the roots of the trees actually curling and growing longer in the earth below. I had the funny feeling that my own feet would change shape and grow roots if I stayed still too long. So I set off.

I walked through the Forest for a long time until

I felt the earth beginning to shake underneath me. I heard a sound like thunder. A crashing and tearing and rumbling. It was terrifying. But I walked on, as bravely as I could. Then, quite soon, I came to the giants.

There were three of them, and they were enormous. They were showing off their magic powers.

The first one – a great, brooding, dark-browed fellow – was changing his shape rapidly into all kinds of creatures: to start with he was a charging bull. Then he became a fiery dragon, then a soaring bird, and then back to his own shape again.

The second one, who was equally hideous, watched the first, but did not seem to be impressed. He practised his own magic. He had the power to make the trees grow at the speed of smoke from a fire. They blossomed and bur-

geoned so fast, that little seedlings became giant oaks in a matter of seconds.

The third giant, who must have been the biggest of the three, was balancing a small, round hat on his head. He obviously thought he was the best, because as soon as his brother had finished making the trees grow, he used his power to turn them to stone.

The whole ferocious business made the Forest shake as if a mighty storm or an earthquake was taking place.

I was about to run for my life when a deep voice boomed out.

"Here, little man, you may help us!" It was the first giant. He had spotted me.

"Me?" I said timidly.

"We have an argument," said the giant.

"We have a disagreement," said the second.

"We have a problem we can't solve," said the

third. This was the one who clutched the hat to his head.

"I – I'll do what I can," I said, but I had to swallow my fear.

"Then decide something for us," went on the first giant. "One of us is more clever than the others. I think it's me, and they think it's them. You were watching us just now. You saw what we can do. Now tell us – who's cleverest?"

I thought quickly. If I said the wrong thing I would have at least two giants pulling me limb from limb.

"I can see that you all have wonderful magic powers," I said.

"That's no answer!" roared the first giant.

"Speak to us properly!" demanded the second.

"We want to know!" thundered the third.

There was no getting out of it. Now was the time to be brave.

"I'll decide," I said. "But first, you have to tell me why you want to know."

"It's easy," replied the first one. "Only the cleverest giant is allowed to wear the hat. He wears it at the moment." He meant the third. "But we all want it. Because underneath that hat lies the Moonstone, and the Moonstone is the most precious thing in the whole Forest!"

This news made my heart jump. Now I had good reason to decide for them.

"If you can change into any living thing," I said to the first giant, "then let me see you change into the little blue crystal that grows by the side of the stream. I can't think of anything better. Can you do that?"

"Of course I can!" he roared. And in the twinkling of an eye he had changed himself into the little blue crystal.

"I forgot to tell him," I said to the other two

48

giants, "that the crystal is not really a living thing, although it grows."

"He should have known that," rumbled the second.

"Now he can't change back," said the third. "He's not so clever."

"That's true," I added. "Well, now – you," I spoke to the second giant, "could do better. You will have to make the trees grow so tightly around you that your brother will never get in to attack you."

"I can easily do that!" he said. And in a flash he made such a thick circle of trees grow up around him, with branches completely woven together, that no one could hear the slightest sound of him.

"Well, he can't get out," I said.

"He's stupid!" observed the third giant. "That leaves me."

"Yes, but you have to prove to me that you have the greatest power of all. Turn the biggest living thing in the world into stone, and I will believe you."

"Ha!" scoffed the giant. "I am the biggest living thing in the world, myself. Just look!" And there and then, he did change himself into stone. A great stone mountain, as a matter of fact. And to this very day, if you go to the Forgotten Forest, there's a place where you can see an enormous stone mountain, and beneath it, a huge ring of trees that you could never get through. And if you looked for it, you would find a tiny blue crystal, growing by the side of a little stream.

That was my doing, and I can still hardly believe that I did it. I found the hat at the top of the mountain.

Under the hat was the Moonstone. I didn't want the hat. The precious stone was silvery coloured, with milky white streaks in it. You could almost see through it, but not quite.

I had no idea how it would help me. But I knew that with the Moonstone in my hands I would find my way to the Seven Magic Marbles and the Dwarf King!

6 The Dwarf King

"But, Grandpa," I said, "how could the Dwarf King be worse than the giants?"

"I think the answer to that is cleverness," replied Grandpa. "Size doesn't really matter. Not when it comes to bad deeds, at least. But you haven't met the Dwarf King yet."

"I don't think I want to either. Grandpa, what made him so bad?"

"That's a hard question to answer. Probably, if he had been good, he would have been very, very good. But he wasn't. He was the opposite. The Dwarf King wouldn't stop at anything. Don't you want to hear about him?"

"Oh, yes!"

"I think I had got to the top of the mountain..."

"And you had found the Moonstone."

"Yes. Well, now, let me see –

From the top of the mountain, I could see right over the Forgotten Forest, to where a stern, black castle stood on a ridge. I knew immediately this was the home of the Dwarf King.

I took my bearings and travelled all day in that

direction. As I came closer, I began to feel a fierce heat on my skin. When I came out of the trees at last, I saw that the castle was not just black any more, but that a bright red wall of fire was surrounding it, in a huge ring.

There was no way through. I thought this was the end. I had failed.

I sat down and gazed at the Moonstone. The princess appeared to me again at that moment, just as her reflection had appeared when I had gazed into the stream. It was her true image again, but this time in the Moonstone. She said to me, "Berry, you have to throw the Moonstone into the fire!" Then she disappeared.

I couldn't bring myself to do it. The old man had said the Moonstone would help me. How could it help me if I threw it away?

The princess appeared again, and said once more, "You must do it, Berry, or I will be lost forever!"

This time I did what she said. I hurled the stone into the wall of fire. There, where it had passed through, an opening appeared, just large enough for me to enter. I darted through the gap. As soon as I was on the other side, the wall of fire closed behind me.

I hoped I would find the Moonstone again. There it was! It lay on the flagstones in the castle entrance. It was not harmed at all. But, instead of its silvery white colour, it was now filled with a soft golden light, like the warmth of the sun.

The castle itself was empty. No living creature stirred. I walked through it, until I came to a dining-hall with a great high ceiling and wooden walls. I sat down at the table and waited.

I had no plan but I had no fears either. I think I had changed too, by going through the ring of fire.

After a while the door creaked open. I expected to see the Dwarf King, but it wasn't – it was an enor- mous black dog, with pointy ears and a stud- ded collar. It stared at me. I could not help looking into its black eyes and, the more I looked, the fainter I felt. I thought I would faint away completely if I stared any longer. So I fixed my eyes on the Moonstone instead, and let its light warm me.

Now a minute later, the Dwarf King himself entered. He was black and twisted like an old gnarled tree-trunk. And yet, to my surprise, he was not particularly small. In fact, he seemed to change size. At one point he looked as big as the room itself. I could not make up my mind what shape or size he really was.

But one thing was clear to me immediately. The Dwarf King had been out in the world and his wicked magic had made the princess sick.

"He glared at me and growled, "Who are you? What do you want?"

I had learned to think quickly so I had a reply

ready.

"Your Majesty," I began, "I really want to learn magic. I've heard that you know more than anyone else. Would you teach me how to be a magician too?"

He peered at me closely, with an evil eye. I thought he would see through me immediately. "If you want to learn magic properly," replied the Dwarf King, "you will have to pass three tests. You've passed the first one already by coming through my wall of fire, though I don't know how you did it. The second test is easier. Do you see that hat hanging on a hook above the fire?"

"I do."

"If you fetch me down that hat you'll have passed the second test. It's the hat I wear when I go out into the world and I will be going out again soon."

He turned on his heels and left the room. The

dog stayed put.

The hat looked surprisingly like the one the giant had worn. It was not very high. I thought I could get it by climbing onto the mantelpiece. But every time I went near the fireplace, the dog barred my way, growling fiercely. Its black eyes burned into my flesh.

At that point I remembered the berries I had stuffed in my pockets. I knew them well, or at least the ones at home which looked the same. The purple ones were for sleeping, the green ones for staying awake. Animals were usually careful about what they ate, but I had a feeling the dog with the black eyes would be interested in these berries. I put the purple ones down in front of him. He sniffed at them at first, then started to lick, and finally ate them up. A minute later his eyelids began to grow very heavy. Soon he was fast asleep. I jumped up and brought

down the hat.

After a while the Dwarf King came back.

"I see you know more than I thought," he said.

"The third task is even easier and should give you no trouble. Follow me."

He led me through a great hall with pillars. Hidden in the pillars were faces, and the shape of arms and legs. I followed him up to a bed-chamber, which had a huge four-poster bed in it, with a heavy wooden canopy or roof.

"There is your third task," said the King. "I told you there was nothing to it. You simply have to sleep there tonight and in the morning tell me your dreams."

He left me alone. I was very tired. I hadn't slept since I was on the Island of Yesterday. I would have been quite happy to try the test and tell him my dreams in the morning. But how could I trust someone like that?

I lay down on the bed. It was like sinking into a cloud of feathers. I desparately wanted to go to sleep. I knew I shouldn't.

I took a handful of the green berries from my pocket and swallowed them. Berry was my name, and my knowledge of herbs and fruits would save me. I crawled behind the bed and sat on the hard stone floor. That night I didn't sleep a wink.

Here I was, still in a fairy-tale world. I was in a castle belonging to an evil Dwarf King. Anything was possible. In the middle of the night his dark magic started to work. The heavy wooden canopy of the four-poster started to move. It was slipping silently down, with all its great weight, onto the bed. A minute later it pressed down on the covers so heavily that anyone who had been lying there would have been crushed to death. Then it sprang up and rose to its proper place.

It was a long night for me, sitting there on the cold flagstones. But I didn't dare go to sleep after that.

In the morning I heard the Dwarf King coming down the corridor. I jumped into the bed and, when he opened the door, I was there, stretching and yawning as if I had been asleep all night.

He looked startled.

"Tell me, then," he demanded, "what dreams you have had."

I had my answer ready.

"I dreamed that a whale swallowed me up in its huge mouth. But my dear mother prayed for me so hard that I was saved!"

"That is an unusual dream!" hissed out the Dwarf King. "Prayers like that have never been heard of in my castle before."

"I'm glad to be safe," I added. "Now will you teach me your magic?"

"You have nothing to learn!" he answered, with a sneer. "If you have the prayers of your mother you don't need magic! Now get out of my castle before it's too late!"

I could hear the sound of horses neighing outside. There was the clattering of hooves, and carriage-wheels on stone. I also heard the roaring of a lion.

"You see, I'm on my way to take over the nearest kingdoms to mine," went on the Dwarf King. "And nothing can stop me. There is a princess who will be mine. She is already in my power. Every night I am there in her dreams and she can do nothing about it."

It was horrible to think of this evil King going in and out of a person's dreams like that and stopping them from waking up. But he wasn't lying. I had to find the Seven Magic Marbles! Only the sun's first rays, dancing on the Seven Magic Marbles, could break the spell of the Dwarf King.

The lion roared again.

"That beast is my little pet," snarled the Dwarf King. "He is waiting for you. Don't you want to meet him?"

"Take me to the Seven Magic Marbles!" I cried.

The Dwarf King looked alarmed for the first time.

"I will not do that!" he answered.

"I you don't take me, I will destroy you with the power of the Moonstone!"

"The Moonstone?!" he laughed. "You should learn to know your enemy better than that. I made the Moonstone!"

I knew more than he thought.

"The Moonstone is filled with the light of the sun. It has the love of the princess in it, and it has been through your wall of fire. It can't be used for evil any more. It can destroy you!"

"Let me see!"

I took out the precious stone. Its warm light flowed through the chamber. The Dwarf King gasped. He seemed to shrink before it and tremble.

"You are a greater magician than I thought," he said in a small voice. "I will take you to the Seven Magic Marbles."

I followed him down through the hall of the pillars. He took me through a secret doorway which led down to passageways undisturbed for centuries. The Dwarf King's eyes gleamed. Cobwebs brushed my face. Bats darted through my hair. I almost turned round and ran. I think this was what the Dwarf King wanted. He never really believed I would reach the Seven Magic Marbles. But I held the Moonstone in front of me, and its pure light guided me. The eyes of the Dwarf King glowed furiously. He seemed to shrink even more. At last we came to an underground vault, far below the castle.

The Dwarf King stopped there. He stood still in front of a loose flagstone.

"Under there!" he hissed.

I lifted the heavy flagstone and slid it across the
ground. It smelled of earth underneath. I saw a
small casket and reached down my hand to lift it.
But as I did so I heard a screech from above. I
turned and saw a black bird flying down. Its

wings flapped against me as if it would push me into the hole under the ground. It was like a horrid shadow trying to blind me. I reached for the Moonstone but my hand passed right through it. The Moonstone was dissolving! The Dwarf King was my enemy. He was the bird.

My hand slid down and knocked open the casket. A bright ray of light flashed out through the vault. The Dwarf King screeched and fell down. His power was gone. The casket lay open. There they were: the Seven Magic Marbles! Their light withdrew again back into the casket. The Moonstone was completely gone.

I lifted the Marbles. I felt completely protected by their light. I didn't care who was there any more. It didn't matter. The Dwarf King's castle was vanishing. The pillars in the great hall turned to light. All the princes and noblemen who had been trapped inside them left their prison and vanished into the light and air.

I don't know if they were dead and going to heaven, but it seemed like that to me.

7 The Seven Magic Marbles

I floated away from the castle too, but I was still alive. I was going under the Forgotten Forest. I recognised the roots. I had seen them in the ground when I had first arrived here. They were even more transparent now, and I was able to

pass through them.

The next moment I was inside the Moonstone. I knew it by the milky colour and the egglike shape. It was flying, with me inside it, over the sea.

I recognized the island I had been on. The old Ferryman waved to me. He was standing right beside me, too, as if he could be in two places at once.

"You have found the Seven Magic Marbles!" he said. "The island is now called 'Tomorrow', because the Marbles have been kept hidden at 'Midnight' for hundreds of years."

But I was already speeding away from him. I had the casket of the Marbles in my hands. I was going in the direction of my thoughts. That means that what I was thinking of was where I was going. Can you understand that? It's like thinking of somewhere so strongly that you just go there. I can't make it much clearer. I was going to the castle. But I was thinking of the princess.

So there I was, immediately before the first light of dawn. The room was dark and still. The princess was lying in bed. I knelt beside her and heard her shallow breathing. I must have prayed for a long time because, when I opened my eyes, the night had gone. The first rays of the

75

morning sun shone through the window.

I opened the casket. The sun's rays glanced on the Seven Magic Marbles and sent coloured reflections dancing through the whole room. Their light fell on the princess's pillow. I saw the little orange flower. I saw her face and golden hair.

The Seven Magic Marbles woke her.

"You did find them," she said. "I knew you would.

"-And that's the end of my story," said Grandpa suddenly.

"But, Grandpa!" I exclaimed. "Didn't you like the princess?"

"Did I like her!? Her eyes were brighter than the Seven Magic Marbles and the Moonstone put together..." His voice trailed off and I saw that his eyes were moist again.

"But, Grandpa," I repeated, "the King said anyone who brought back the Seven Magic Marbles would marry the princess and have half the kingdom for himself. Didn't you do that?"

"I think that Berry did."

"But you said you were Berry!"

"Yes, I was. Let me explain –

The idea of the princess never left me after that. But I felt I had to go back to the crystal cave. I wanted to see the damage the Dwarf King had done. I took the Seven Magic Marbles in my hand.

To my surprise, the lion in the cage was exactly where I had first seen it. I let the lion out. The woods and mountains there were full of lions and bears, so one more would not make much difference. It bounded off into the woods and I did not see it again.

The place around the cave was very special, I thought. The ground was covered with moss and pine needles. Wild herbs grew among the rocks. These were the best herbs for making medicines. I walked among them with the Seven Magic Marbles. The sun's rays glanced and danced all around. Then, at last, I went back into the cave itself.

There was a conversation going on between the Seven Magic Marbles and the crystals in the cave. I don't mean they were talking, but the coloured light passed between them, backwards and forwards. Probably the Marbles had been made out of crystals from this cave.

The dancing, coloured light grew stronger and stronger until it was so bright that I felt dizzy again, and must have fainted.

When I woke up I was myself again. I was no longer in another time and another place. I was not Berry any more. I was myself.

"How did you know the difference, Grandpa?" I asked.

"Well, in Berry's time things were still unspoiled. I knew that difference straightaway. I could feel it in myself. I was a different person."

"But, Grandpa, you still had the Seven Magic Marbles!"

"I had these marbles in my hand. I don't believe their magic can quite reach into our times. Maybe if you look very hard at them, or if you're the right person, you might see it. I haven't. The only other thing I have to tell you about, of course, is the princess. I said there was one thing that made me really quite sure the whole thing did happen, and I wasn't dreaming. And that was the idea of the princess. I told you I saw her image in the stream and in the Moonstone. In the same way her true image has stayed alive in me ever since. It may have been Berry who married her and became king, but I know for myself what I saw. How could I ever forget the moment when the first rays of the morning sun danced on the Seven Magic Marbles and the princess awoke!"